Fossil Hunti

Heather Hammonds

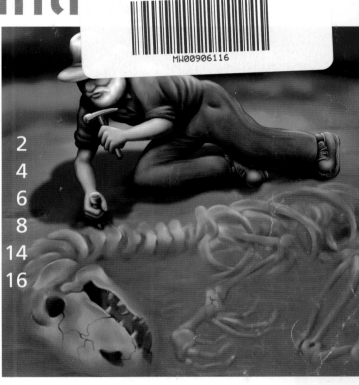

Contents

NELSON

THOMSON LEARNING ™

Australia · Canada · Mexico · Singapore · Spain · United Kingdom · United States

Life Long Ago

Fossils are parts of plants
and animals that lived long ago.

Fossils help us learn
what Earth was once like.

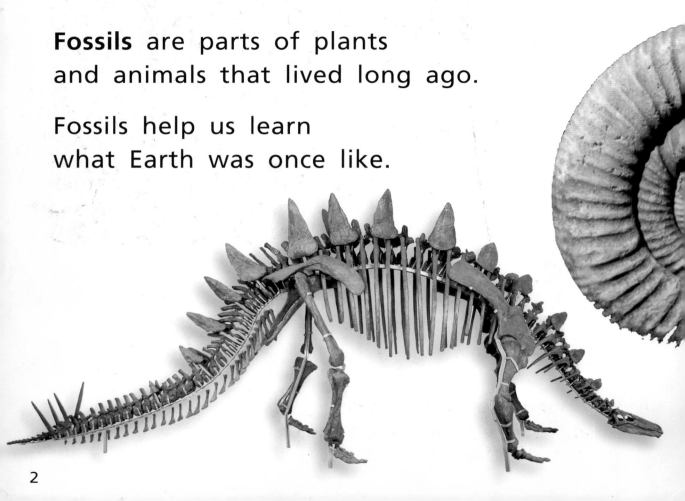

Animal bones, teeth and shells
are many of the fossils found today.

3

How Do Fossils Form?

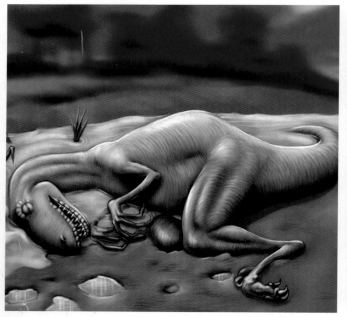

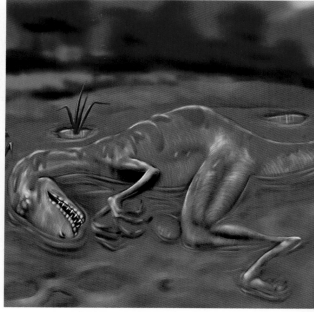

Fossils can form when an animal or plant dies.

When this **dinosaur** died, sand and mud covered it.

Over a long time,
the sand and mud
slowly became rock.

This dinosaur
became a fossil
this way.

Dinosaur Fossils

Dinosaur fossils are found in rocks.

The word dinosaur means 'terrible lizard', but not all dinosaurs were big monsters. Some dinosaurs were quite small!

Fossil Hunting

People who dig up and study fossils are called **palaeontologists.**

Palaeontologists work together at **fossil sites.**

At fossil sites, rocks are broken up
to see if there are any fossils inside them.
This is long, hard work.
Sometimes, a whole skeleton is found!

Special tools are used
to get fossils out of rocks.
It is very slow work.

Palaeontologists
must be very careful
not to break the fossils.

This fossil was put in plaster to keep it safe.

Some fossils are sent to **museums.**
Palaeontologists study the fossils carefully.

Some fossils are put on show.
Everyone can see them, and learn about
plants and animals from long ago.

Fossil Timeline

Different animals
and plants lived
on Earth
at different times.

550 – 245 million years ago

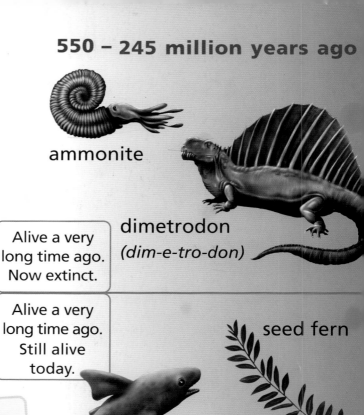

ammonite

dimetrodon
(dim-e-tro-don)

Alive a very
long time ago.
Now extinct.

Alive a very
long time ago.
Still alive
today.

seed fern

shark

dragonfly

14

245 – 65 million years ago

dinosaur

archaeopteryx
(ar-key-op-ter-ix)

65 million years ago – Today

eohippus
(ee-o-hip-us)

woolly
mammoth

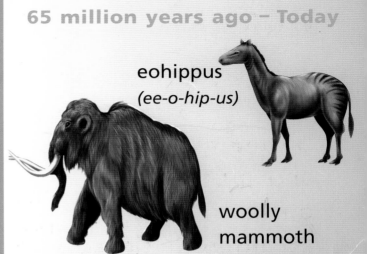

snake   flower

frog

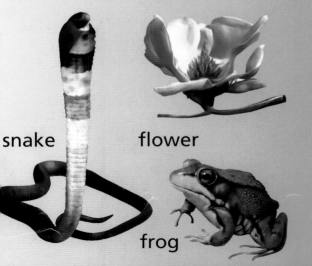

bat   chimpanzee

whale

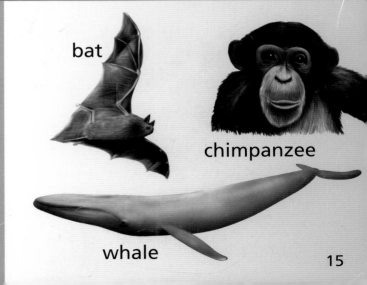

Glossary

dinosaur an animal that lived on Earth many millions of years ago

fossils parts of animals and plants from long ago

fossil sites places where fossils are found

museums buildings where interesting things are kept, for everyone to see. Some of these things are very old.

palaeontologists scientists who dig up and study fossils